ABOUT THE AUTHOR

It has been my heart's desire to write since I can remember. As a young girl and through out my adolescence there was nothing that could compare to curling up on my bed and writing poetry or short stories. I could escape all reality and travel to far away places and different times. I would become a part of the very works that I created. The words just flowed from my pen then, never ending; they brought me so much enjoyment. I kept two large folders of my work and only allowed certain family members such as my parents to read them. My Father had always wanted to be a cartoonist, but his work led him far away from this dream. For fun he sent away for drawing assessment tests, which he always did very well at. He tried to encourage me to not let my dreams to write pass me by.

He died rather suddenly when I was almost 19. To this day I miss him dearly. I didn't heed his advice and soon work and family consumed all of my time. Never the less, I still never found the time to write. I was very fortunate though to spend a lot of time with my children as they grew up, as my work was home-based. I have always shared their love of fantasy in books and movies. My children are all grown now, and I am finally able to pursue my writing. At last I can go into the far recesses of my mind and become that youthful girl again, that loved to put her thoughts on paper. My only hope is that the reader will thoroughly enjoy this book as much as I have enjoyed creating it.

INTRODUCTION

The Lands of Nod is a fantasy book for all ages, with many characters and turns and twists to it. It is the beginning of a trilogy. It is a never-ending story at this moment, which I intend to two books to, each pursuing the adventures of a different character from the original book. As a matter of fact I have already begun writing the second book just recently.

CHAPTER ONE

THE MYSTERY BEGINS

Far, far away beyond the foaming 7 seas, beneath the countless glistening stars, in the endless eternal skies, imbedded in the realms of unconsciousness lies the timeless ever-changing lands of Nod. Surrounded by a fierce raging ocean, covered in a dreamy mist, the land holds many tales of lore and mystery. She is filled with the gurgles of sparking mountain streams, lush green rolling hills, grassy knolls, craggy cliffs, majestic mountains, barren wastelands and deep forests of whispering pines. You cannot travel there by land, or by sea, only by way of the deep abyss of your unconsciousness, through the tunnels and passages of your dreams, beyond the realms of reality, deep in the shadows of fantasy. Your journey will bring you upon the many awesome wonders, creatures and beasties of Nod; wherein resides the Horks (a very distant relative to the leprechaun).

These wee people make their homes from the hollowed out trunks of the forest trees. Something, which is abundantly, provided them thanks to the swiftness of the mighty lumberjack's ax. The leader of the clan is Bjork, which casts an uncanny resemblance to a wizard both in physical aspects and mental wisdom. A man of frail stature with a pointed chin and nose to match and deep set pale blue eyes, that light up and sparkle when he is spinning a tale of the past or asked an interesting question. He is cloaked in the long green gown which Naomi the Nimbus Fairy Princess gave to him as a gift long ago. It is said that the gown has powers of it's own that have protected Bjork from many an evildoer. His gown is faded and tattered at the hem; a few patches have been loving placed here and there over the many years. The gown has the miraculous ability to cleanse itself daily and therefore it is not necessary to wash it. This is Bjork's most treasured possession. It is said that he puts it under lock and key while attending to his bathing ritual, (the only time that he is without it). It would be a most vulnerable time for Bjork as one of his adversaries could make an attempt to harm or slay him. Therefore he never bathes at the same time of day.

As has been told for many years Bjork and Naomi were at one time long ago lovers. It was a sad fate the day the two decided that their love was in vain. Naomi being a Nimbus fairy was beautiful as are all the other fairies, each having their own individual special coloring and appearance. Every color of the rainbow was represented in their glistening hair, with their beautiful fairy wings that matched in color. Glistening blues eyes and red smiling lips they enchanted the viewer with their presence. But alas along with their breath-taking beauty they were cursed with an everlasting youth, or so it seemed to the mortals. As Bjork grew older and showed the signs of age, the tell-tell wrinkles of the forehead, the crinkles around the eyes, the graying and thinning of his hair, Naomi remained as young as beautiful as ever. Fairies age at such a slow rate that a mere second of their time is worth a year of a mortal. Even with their massive knowledge of magic and spells they couldn't change their fate. So sadly they vowed to remain best of friends until Bjork the Hork was no more but the center of tales of yore told around the Hork fireside. True to her promise Naomi remained his very best friend and advisor in times of strife and war.

 Naomi stood a whole 6 1/2 inches tall at most times and could become Hork size with the flutter of her beautiful wings. She had hair of the most golden yellow and matching shimmering wings and the deepest blue eyes and a small pouty mouth. She led the Nimbus Fairies with true authority, and her kind gentle loving nature commanded and won their respect. They would often help the Horks with their daily tasks such as spinning the fine gold fibers for their fishing nets.

 The Horks main diet was the fruits and nuts of the forest and the small minnows they caught from the sparkling streams. It was truly an all day effort for a crew of ten Horks to catch the fish for the monthly allotment. Hoisting the net carefully as a team they toiled all day casting and retrieving their catch. It was laborious work and as they struggled and sweat they sang of the old man and the sea. Their wives with cherub type features, stout, a little plump with round jolly faces, and rosy cheeks would slave away cooking the evening meal. It too was a very laborious task, stacking the wood and hanging the large vat above the flames. They sang songs of fellowship as they took turns stirring the pot. The children raced and played hide and seek among the forest ferns. The return of the victorious males with their hefty catch of glistening trout would cause such a stir of activity.

They were friends with all the forest animals and beasties and the birds often helped them carry their heavy-laden net brimming with fish back to the village. The children would rush to greet them and stand in awe as the net was spread open upon the ground. Then the wives proceeded to reward their husbands with a cheerful peck upon their stubbly cheeks, as they hastened to scatter the breadcrumbs for the birds evening feast. The fish were all to be cleaned and hung in strips very carefully in the nearby smokehouse. A large wooden structure made of strong timber and topped with a clay brick smokestack. The flue always remained open when the fire had been started. There was an open side for easy access to stoking the flames with fuel. Only during emergency, such as when the wee Horks tossed cedar in the fire (which the older Horks knew was not the type of wood meant for smoking meats.)

was the flue shut to prevent the fish from scorching. The smell of smoked fish would fill the air for days after.

The houses were constructed from the large hollow base of trees, with steps that led down into the ground, into somewhat of an underground cave. The sod and dirt insulated their structures and kept them cool in the summer and warm in the winter. On the top floor, which led to the front door, was a sitting room with beautiful hand carved furniture and a large clay brick fireplace. Each tree stump (house) had a chimney that rose from the top and on cold nights in the forest you could see the rising of little puffs of smoke from all over the forest floor. Below in the cavern there was winding pathways and secret chambers, where the Horks kept their most valued possessions. Their friends the moles had helped them burrow through the dirt and construct these beautiful mazes underground. Each room had a different function, some for reading, (they were fantastic tale spinners and writers), some for sleeping, some for visitors and some for conversing. They did all of their eating outside around the community fire. The women would wash the dishes in the nearby streams as the men sat and smoked their wooden pipes and told tall tales. The children would bathe in the creek and toddled off to bed as the sun fell and the forest grew dark. Sometimes they would sit out late around the fire and drink the ancient grog that their father's had taught them to brew. A tasty and strong concoction made from fermented berries. They would retire when the last flask had been emptied and the fire had long gone out.

It was upon a day such as this that Bjork began one of his most fascinating adventures. He had had his fill of the wonderful evening meal the women had made, fish stew, and a large plate of nuts and berries, and washed it all down with some grog. He was feeling tired and decided it was time for him to take his daily bath. He returned home and carefully locked the door behind him. He descended the stairs and wound his way through the many familiar paths, entering the library with the countless volumes of books he had written, he bent down on his knees and opened the bottom door beneath the bottom shelf. Then he rose and carefully untied the belt around his waist and let the green gown drop to the floor. He immediately retrieved it stooped down and placed it inside the wooden door. He reached up to the center shelf and opened the largest book and inside the hollowed out cover laid a wooden key. He grabbed the key shut the wooden door and carefully locked it with the key. He returned the key with a sigh to it's book, muttering "If only life were more simple, I wouldn't need to take such measures as these for a simple bath" He then stumbled off naked and weary to the pathway and begin his ascent. When he reached the sitting room he grabbed the blanket off the wooden rocker and wrapped it around his waist.

 He threw open the door and stepped onto the forest floor. It felt cool beneath his bare feet as he traveled by starlight to the nearby stream. The children had long retired, and the women chose to bathe during the daytime, while they took turns watching the children. So completely confident that he would be unseen, his steps began to pick up in stride. He even had a little spring in each step and a smile upon his face, as he reminisced of Naomi and listened to the cheerful sounds of the gurgling waters. When he reached the stream, he hastily disrobed and slipped into the swirling waters. Their warmth was a mystery, even to the Nimbus fairies. No matter what time of day or night, or what season of the year, they remained peacefully warm and soothing. He was humming to himself and thoroughly enjoying the moment, when he heard a rustling in the ferns. He stopped humming to get a better grasp on the noise he had heard. It was strangely silent. He didn't hear the forest owls, the raccoons, or any other nocturnal beast. Pure silence. That's strange he thought and a cold shiver ran up his spine. He shrugged it off and continued bathing. In the distance he could see the men's evening fire and it left him with a sense of security and peace. As he was once again feeling happy, he heard the rustles louder than ever. "Who may it be? He asked", "Be ya friend or be ya foe?"

There was no reply as the eerie silence again returned. Once again he implored, a little louder this time" Be ya friend or be ya foe? The words had but left his mouth when the rustling grew very loud and the answer to his question became very apparent. The scent came first in little wisps on the breeze and as the thing grew nearer it engulfed him and grew as a huge cloud around his nostrils. It gagged him as he gasped deeply in fear. He tried to hold his breath as the stench began to nauseate him. Then the ferns parted and out stepped the grotesque, snarling beast. The smell of rotten flesh filled the air, as it towered over the edge of the stream, peering down upon Bjork with its evil glowing eyes. Its long yellow pointed teeth were spaced crookedly inside its huge mouth, which dripped with saliva. It's hair was long and matted and covered 99 percent of the beast. (Everything but the soles of its huge flat feet, and the palms of its large clawed hands.) A troll! Bjork wanted to scream, but his mouth wouldn't open, as he trembled and shivered with fear. The warm waters of the stream felt icy and cold now, as he struggled to think of a way out of his plight. He had no weapons and could never outrun the long strides from the legs of his adversary. He wasn't that avid a swimmer, (adequate,) but at his age he had no hopes of swimming down stream any distance. Besides the troll could run much faster on shore and catch him when he grew tired of swimming, and tried to make his way ashore. He was wishing with all his might that he had his green gown now, (without it he had no powers to dispel the beast.)

In one long swoop the troll reached over and made a grab for Bjork, he dived beneath the waters and held his breath. Perhaps if I hold my breath long enough it will tire and go away assuming I've perished, he thought. But Bjork was an old man and he couldn't hold his breath for long. He may very well die trying. Oh well drowning would be a far better death than at the hands of this beast. At that very second there was a tremendous splash; the waters were pulsating with ripples from the weight that created it. He startled and began to take water in his lungs as with natural instinct he rose towards the surface, gasping for air until his head emerged.

There on the shore stood Nimrod (Naomi's brother) with a huge smile of gallantry, he replied. "I happened upon you at quite the right time I see". Nimrod was a tall handsome fairy with hair of golden blonde and deep friendly blue eyes. Many a female nimbus fairy had been smitten by his charm, yet he remained content in his bachelor lifestyle, and truly adored and worshiped his older sister Naomi. The two were inseparable friends. Bjork had taken a liking to him instantly. The nimbus fairies had conquered many a troll with their swift flight and true shot with their arrows that always found the vulnerable spot to pierce the flesh of the troll. Right between the eyes, there was a very thin layer of skin; the skull underneath was open there leaving the brain exposed. With the slightest pierce and high accuracy the arrow would enter the brain and the Troll would succumb to death. It was a swift and painless death, as the fairies were a peaceful people and hated to cause pain or anguish. Thus Nimrod had successfully slain the troll that had planned on Bjork for his evening repast. The loud splash had been the beast falling into the water after Nimrod's arrow had pierced its brain with his sure aim.

The Nimbus fairies were forced for many centuries to fight the evil Trolls, which feasted upon their like and the Hork's. Bjork was very surprised to see Nimrod, especially with an unannounced visit and inquired" Why is it that ye happened upon me like this tonight?" "Surely it tis my lucky day". You're a very welcome sight to these old eyes indeed".

" There is a matter of utmost urgency he replied, your wisdom is required, and your sworn secrecy also. I know no other as wise nor as trustworthy as Bjork the Hork; therefore I must beseech you to hasten as the time already draws near."

"What time draws near? What is the matter?"Bjork asked.

"Shush Bjork be patient I will tell you all, but not here, you must come tonight to Naomi's meadow, there in fairy protection, I will reveal all."
Naomi's Meadow was a most beautiful and alluring part of The Land of the Nimbus Fairies.It had always been Naomi's favorite place to be as a fairy child. Her Father Caliope (being the King) had named it for her in a gesture of deep affection upon her reaching fairy adolescence. It was a favorite spot for Bjork to visit also. For it was here that he had told her first of his undying love for her, a love that he still bore today. In Naomi's Meadow it is said that nothing can enter besides the forest animals, the fairies and their guests, and beyond it's walls their voices cannot be heard by anyone.

As mysteriously as he appeared Nimrod vanished into a blue twinkling haze that traveled quickly and disappeared in the now rolling thick fog.
In haste Bjork sprang from the water grabbed his blanket and wrapped it securely around his dripping aged body. The fog was growing ever so much thicker and it was becoming very difficult to see the path in front of him. He hastened his pace down the familiar walk, one he had taken so many times before. He didn't need to see; he could find his way back in total darkness, so familiar was the feel of it's trodden dirt beneath his toes and the sounds of the night that followed him. He could hear the owls in the trees and feel the gentle breeze upon his face. Sooner than he anticipated he had reached that well-known stump

with the large carved wooden door. Ah home sweet home he mused. Then he stepped inside to the cheerful glow from his fireplace, and proceeded to his library to retrieve his precious green gown. He always felt so naked without it! In no time he had removed it from it's hiding place and slipped it over his body. Once again he felt the powers from the gown as it relinquished his body with the memories of his youth. He felt years younger, although the mirror would tell him something quite to the contrary. Than he realized that he must hurry to Naomi's meadow, as the evening was growing very late and with the thick fog that had rolled in, he must use the powers of the gown to transport his body there. It was one of the most wonderful of the gown's powers. In a flash with just a simple thought pertaining to where he wished to travel, he could appear anywhere instantaneously within the Hork land. It was very useful for nights such as these and saved him from many a fateful malady while escaping the clutches of an enemy. So with his head bowed and in deep thought he traveled mentally to Naomi's meadow, as he raised his arms in a triumphant sweeping motion he was instantly transported there. He stood and took in the beauty of it all, the meadow that held no time, no place, always full of light, never darkness. He was enjoying the smell of the flowers and watching the fairies frolicking in the woods, when Nimrod once again appeared.

By the somber look upon his face Bjork could see that this matter was a very serious one indeed. He began to grow nervous as he waited for Nimrod to speak. Slowly and carefully Nimrod began, "Bjork, it is with the utmost urgency that I must inform you of this matter. Naomi lies in deep slumber and cannot be awakened as she is approaching the time of her mortality. She will surely die unless we succeed at this dangerous mission."

Two fortnights have passed since the awful moment that seized her in this dreadful fate. She had gone out in search of special flowers for a bouquet that she wished to present to Bjork on the anniversary of their first encounter. Having traveled far into the land of the Trolls to gather the rare and beautiful flowers that only grow in that region, she had grown very weary. She stopped to rest upon the dead stump of an ancient tree, stretched herself out upon its surface and was just beginning to rest. It was at this moment that a deadly Boringo wasp that had been watching from above decided to invade her peaceful rest, (out of curiosity), for even Nimbus fairies rarely are seen in this land. It's loud buzzing startled Naomi and when she sprang to her feet one of her wings glanced the tip of its protruding stinger. The pain was severe and poor Naomi lay upon the stump trembling for it grew too intense for her to move. At that time a DODO bird heard her sighs and being of a friendly species flew closer to assess the situation. He called to her in his peculiar screeching and Naomi replied as only fairies can, for they are capable of speaking to all creatures in their native tongues. She told the Dodo of her tragic encounter with the Boringo and in no time the friendly Dodo had swooped her up with one wing and placed her upon his strong back. He proceeded then to carry her back to the Nimbus fairy meadow. Somewhere along the way she fell into the deep slumber and it was Nimrod and 4 other Nimbus fairies, which brought her to rest upon her Lily bed.

Nimrod began conversing with the wise owls of the meadow, in his worried state, and they brought him to the Ancient Tree, (the oldest wisest living tree of Naomi's meadow). He was without a doubt a source of great lore and wisdom to the Nimbus fairies. Centuries old was he and had seen and heard more than any other living creature in Nod. He had grown very old and a little slower to answer these days. So when Nimrod asked him if he knew of a cure for a Boringo wasp sting, his reply was slow and garbled. Nimrod had to ask him to repeat himself a few times as his voice had grown weak and frail with age. He then told him that the only known cure for the Boringo wasp sting came from the juice of the JUJU berry. The JUJU berry grew abundantly in the pastures of LOX.

Lox were terrible beasts, a cross between a lion and an OX. They were huge and swift upon their feet. With sharp claws and long fangs and large Cloven feet. The only route to the pastures of LOX was through the land of the Trolls! A dark and stormy land full of haunted enchanted forests and deep dark stench-filled caves. Covered with thorns and thistles and bogs, steep craggy cliffs and mysterious foggy mountain paths. Very few lived to tell the tales of the land of the Trolls and those who did never returned there, except in their own restless dreams. Men in their greed had ventured to travel there in pursuit of riches, for in the caves it is said the walls are laden with silver and gold. In the mountain streams they say golden nuggets lie as big as a man's fist. The Trolls carefully guard their treasures and patrol the boundaries of their land, lying in wait for the foolish intruders. Many a Troll feast has come from the capture of men such as these.

Nimrod finished explaining Naomi's situation in full details. Bjork, looking extremely sad and overought persisted that Nimrod take him to Naomi immediately. He felt his heart would break in two if he couldn't just lay his eyes upon her once more. Nimrod tried his best to explain that haste was what was needed, and that gazing upon Naomi would do her no good. He tried his best to convince Bjork that the best thing to do was to prepare for their journey to the pastures of LOX at once. But it was to no avail and as he saw the injured look upon Bjork's weary face and the moistening of his eyes. Nimrod was helpless and overwhelmed with pity for his dear friend.

"As ya wish I will take ya there but only for a brief visit ", he said. "As soon as you have seen her we must take our leave, before it's too late. We have no time to waste I remind ya!"

As Bjork gazed down upon Naomi resting so peacefully upon her lily pad bed, which was strewn with the petals of hundreds of red roses (a get well gift the female Nimbus fairies had brought to her), he was choked with emotion. How beautiful she was. Her ageless beauty had always mystified him. It instantly took him back to the day when he had first laid eyes upon her. He felt the passion in his heart rise and couldn't resist bending down to place a kiss upon her delicate mouth. As he lingered there for a moment, her body still, no response to his kiss, her eyes closed, tears began to stream down his face, and drops fell upon her breast. He bent his head and placed it there and could hardly decipher a very faint heartbeat. It was at that moment that he snapped back into reality, and his heart was filled with anger and determination as he spoke.

"Nimrod, we must not tarry here any longer. We must gather our provisions for the journey and leave at once!" Nimrod had been quietly watching Bjork from a distance in respect for his privacy, but when Bjork spoke he sprang into action. He called upon the Nimbus fairy women and told them to gather the necessary food and water for their long journey. (Fairies live on the nectars of sweet blooming flowers and honeycomb), Bjork would need dried fruits and nuts and warm bedding.) Not Nimrod or his fairy men for they never sleep, they only rest. Bjork would call upon the powers of the robe to keep him warm (as it had so many times long ago).

In no time the chattering female fairies surrounded them, each wishing them a safe successful journey. They had gathered all the necessary provisions. Now Nimrod only needed to adjourn the Fairy council. He must call upon the aid of four of the fiercest fighting male fairies. Marksmen in their ability in archery, they must accompany the two as bodyguards. The oldest of the female fairies Harriah placed the golden horn (taken from a LOX beast centuries before) into Nimrod's hand. He solemnly reached for it, held it briefly to his lips and blew. The whole meadow shook with the noise and vibrations that came from this magical horn. The sky became thick with fairy wings and the flutter created a large commotion and winds that almost knocked Bjork off his feet. He never realized how many male fairies there were. It seemed like thousands!

How would Nimrod be able to pick only 4 from these in such a short period of time? His father Calliope the Nimbus Fairy King stood solemn at his side. He was an old and wise fairy man, and in all his many, many years, nothing had pained him so much as to see his daughter Naomi in such a dire situation. His wife Geneva had been stolen away by the Leprechauns so many years before. He had tried many times to find her, and sent hundreds of fairy men out to search. They had traveled through the dark evil land of the Cyclops to the East to the very shores of the fierce raging sea. They had heard tales that Leprechaun Isle was but 200 miles across the sea But not being seamen and not knowing how to plot a course, or how to read a compass, or what the true location of the Isle was, they had given up that quest for another day. They had also heard of a fierce dark pirate that patrolled these waters called One-Eyed Jack. They didn't care to meet up with the likes of him. It was heard that he held twenty fairies captive onboard his ship. Upon this ship lived his sea-witch Hagatha. She had cast an evil spell upon the fairies, which left them powerless. So upon the vessel aptly named The Cursed Crusader they toiled heavily for the pirate night and day. Thus they returned home empty-handed. Caliope did not give up hope. He had been planning to send his fairies out in search of an able seaman, someone capable of traveling to Leprechaun Isle. But for now it must wait, for now he must think only of Naomi.

Naomi bore a very striking resemblance to her beautiful Mother and was all that Caliope had left to remember her by. He was seldom emotional, but perhaps old age or the hopeless way he felt now consumed him. He seemed much more fragile and a lot less like the warrior that Nimrod had known him to be. His wings were bent in submission as he spoke, "Nimrod my son, I would go myself but I no longer have the powers, nor the youth that you possess," (although by appearance he had not seemed to age). Nimbus fairies of his generation, had lost most of their powers, and although he would have a very long life, he would become more dependent upon the younger fairies as time progressed. Until one day he would simply sit and write his memoirs to teach the newest fairy children of their heritage. He would remain a very useful part of the clan, but at that time his crown would be passed on to the more youthful Nimrod, his only son, and rightful heir.

Soon the male fairies landed and stood side by side forming a circle four rows deep. Bjork was amazed by the size of their arms, (which were often concealed by their wings). They had massive chests and biceps and stood tall and lean, the epitome of fairy youth. Nimrod stood in the center of the circle alone with Bjork and called upon Nebucaneezer the oldest and wisest of the fairy men. He appeared in the form of a large blue haze that shrunk to the size of his frail fairy body as it faded and he emerged. He was now withered and bent with age, and had lived for many eons, and foretold of many stories future and past. A fairy of small stature he was dwarfed by the others, there he stood, in his long white silken gown, with his prominent nose, his greatly expanded receding hairline, (yet the hair that flowed from his somewhat large ears back was long gray and silken and flowed to his breast, as well as his long pointed beard.) He also wore a full mustache. All were impeccably groomed.

He carried much dignity and ambiance. He had been such a handsome fairy in his youth (many eons ago), and still the female fairies adored him (young and old) His charisma had not faded at all with his age. He was envied by many a fairy man. He also carried the awesome fairy powers of a wizard and could conjure up any vision upon need or request.

Nimrod waved him nearer and when he was close enough he whispered something in his ear. Nebucaneezer smiled and nodded,

"Hmmm, I see", he said. Then with a mighty swoop of his wings and lifting up of his palms he spoke." Alas my fellow fairy men I have been called upon to help Nimrod choose the 4 most fierce- hearted of you all. It will be in this simple test that the four shall be chosen." He pointed a long frail finger to the hollowed out stump of a large oak tree." Inside this stump you each will go (you only need to remain there for 3 minutes), the 4 who are able to complete this task will accompany Bjork and Nimrod on this perilous journey. An honor beyond compare."

The fairies looked amused as they mumbled. 3 minutes, that's very easily done. But they had no idea of the terrible beasts, and the horrors they would face within that 3 minutes. They would be fighting with the demons of their own mind. For this stump had the magical power of deciphering their fears. Once inside their every nightmare and every fear would come alive and endure for a full 3 minutes. The visions were so realistic in appearance, smell, sound and odor that it was impossible to tell that they were only figments of their imagination.

The fairy men entered one by one and once inside the terrible sounds of fear, and their screaming and groaning became louder and louder until they would emerge in a state of frenzy drenched with sweat and weak from their inner battles, completely drained and fatigued, they would stumble out looking for a place to rest. Some fell as they left the stump and crawled away in shame, others remained as if in a trance and mumbled indistinct words as they stared with disbelief. None lasted more than 2 minutes. It continued on throughout the evening hours.

After several had fallen and none had been chosen, a tall muscular fairy man with curly blonde locks and a moustache called Jacor was sent into the stump. He had been well renowned for his courageous battles with the Cyclops. The swampland of the Cyclops bordered the edges of the Hork forest to the East, (not many Horks nor fairies had traversed that path) yet, the Cyclops were often successful in reaching the boundaries of the Hork's forest. Therefore, Hork and fairy alike carefully guarded it. These Cyclops were hideous beasts towering over 7 feet tall, their arms slung low at their sides (their huge hands almost scraping the earth beneath them), causing them to look in appearance as if hunched over, they had massive backs and thighs, spindly little legs and cumbersome feet. It was surprising how agile they were and how quickly they could scale a tree, or jump over an obstacle in their path. They had very large round baldheads with massive pointed ears and long protruding noses. One huge eye was placed in the middle of their forehead (which often scanned hurriedly from left to right); they had a very keen sense of smell for Hork in particular. They lived in harmony with the Trolls who often traded them treasures in return for captured Horks. It was said that Jacor had slew over 25 of them just this past winter.

As Jacor entered the hollow stump the sounds that omitted from there were haunting, evil, screams and screeches, but his voice remained silent. Nebucaneezer glanced at his pocket watch, carefully scrutinizing the elapsed time as he had with all that had past before. He had a quizzical and puzzled expression on his face as he patiently waited for the 3 minutes to pass. The remaining fairy men also waited, wondering what horrors they would meet when it came to be their turn. Slowly and seriously Nebucaneezer snapped the pocket watch shut and called "Time!" Out stepped Jacor covered with sweat and triumphant, wearing a peaceful smile upon his strong face. A rousing cheer of hurrah arose in the night as all congratulated him on his victory. Once again the testing began and as before all the fairy men failed to last for 3 minutes.

About an hour had passed since Jacor's victory, when a dark haired stocky muscular fairy man called Ryob emerged from the crowd and took his turn in the stump. His tendency towards tipping the ale (a little too often I daresay), and his reputation as an excellent bedfellow with the fairy women was well known. He was said to have a fiery temper if crossed and a sure aim. Once again the eerie smells and sounds occurred and once again Nebucaneezer carefully monitored the progress on his pocket watch. A very jovial and triumphant Ryob emerged and sat by Jacor's side. More cheering and then the testing resumed. It was quite some hours later when the last two were chosen,

Jeziah a fair-haired fairy man with a very sharp inquisitive mind (a true genius at strategic problem solving), and Mahew a dark haired swarthy fairy with a creative talent for drawing, (his pictures literally coming to life).

As the sun began to rise over the horizon the splendor of the Victorious 4 was fully visible to all. How magnificent they looked standing there side by side, the finest of all fairiedom. Ah yes, at last it was done and now the journey could begin. Bjork was amazed at their splendor and size and truly pleased with the method that Nebuccaneezer had chosen for selecting these fine specimens. He knew by instinct that along with Nimrod, these 4 and the wonderful powers of his gown, there would be no question but to succeed in obtaining the cure for his dear Naomi. Fired by this newfound confidence Bjork felt renewed, he felt refreshed and more than ready to start the journey, (although he hadn't slept all night).

CHAPTER TWO

ON THE ROAD

Nebuccaneezer offered quick blessings to the courageous travelers as they began to assemble their belongings for the journey. Nimrod would lead with Jacor. Bjork and Ryob would follow, and Jeziah and Mahew would take up the end. Caliope was there also and stepped forward from the crowd to say," Nimrod my son you are my only hope, I know I can depend on you to return with Naomi's cure." "Bjork I too know that you have loved my daughter deeper than any soul that exists, this will give me comfort as I await news of your victory." I know in my heart that love will save my daughter and with so much love between you both, I cannot see any room for failure". Go with the blessings of all the Nimbus fairies and Godspeed your safe return!" He turned his back and Nimrod swore he could see him wipe away a tear as he walked away into the distance.

The day had dawned into a perfect Hork day. Sun shining and cloudless blue skies as the group began their travels. They first came upon the Sparking streams of Wisteria a small Hork village leading to the barren rocky wastelands of Endure. It was odd how beautiful this place was, it was such a stark contrast to the neighboring land of Endure. The sparking streams would fill their empty water flasks, a necessity for the next leg of their journey. The forest was teeming with life and the cheerful laughter of the Hork children at play, caused Bjork to feel a longing for what he was leaving behind. Endure was an odd neighboring wasteland so dreary, empty and vast.

Many had pondered as to what had caused Endure to perish.
It is said that in days of yore it was filled with green valleys and sparkling streams and lush pastures. But an evil had befallen it and now nothing could live, nor anything could grow upon its soil. Sooner than they would have liked they came upon its border. Endure was such a barren waste, so dry and dusty and lifeless. The days were hot and dry, and the nights bitterly cold. No shelter, no food, no water. Travelers had to be wary of this and bring along the necessary food and

drink to survive. It was best to travel in the daylight. Although it was extremely hot, during the day, the dangerous rocky cliffs were easier to travel. It was a good 6 hours journey from the border of Endure to the land of the Trolls.

Wearily they began their journey through this strange eerie land. It was a long and arduous trip climbing the rugged cliffs and scaling the barren hills. There was never a sign by sight, sound or smell of another living creature. Not the slightest hint of a small green stem. Total devastation for as far as the eyes could see. They hastened their way through this land with the eerie feeling of something lurking behind them in a shadow watching their every move. The sun was beginning to set upon the western ridge when they finally could see a change in the landscape. There lying ahead of them perhaps a mile or so was a dense green forest of tall pine trees. They took a brief rest at that time and ate a small repast and drank a little water waiting for the final rays to sink beyond the horizon. At last they were approaching the Land of the Trolls. They knew it was far better to travel there at night. The Trolls had very poor vision at night and relied upon their sense of smell. The Horks had brought along fish oil to cover themselves (they knew the Trolls hated the smell of fish), therefore the smell would work as a Troll repellent. It was odd how sensitive the Trolls were to other smells, when they themselves reeked of such a terrible odor. With the help of his fairy friends Bjork would be silently flown above ground to leave no sign of intruders. Jacor and Ryob each grabbed an arm with careful precision as Bjork became airborne. He loved flying with the fairies; everything looked and felt so magical from this point of view.

It was pitch black inside the Troll forest, as the fairies made their way, carefully listening for the sounds of danger and the familiar sickening stench of the Trolls. They could hear the owls up in the branches above them and the sounds of the Skinks that scurried on the ground amongst the dead branches and leaves. Skinks were a distant relative of the Armadillo, and only ventured out after dark to consume whatever insects they might find. They were completely harmless to all other living creatures, but their appearance could frighten even the most stouthearted.

In this mysterious forest there lived the Wimpets, a wee people who had taken to living under ground many centuries ago. It is said that they lived in grand style in a maze of curving paths, a virtual underground city. There they were safe to carry on their daily tasks far beneath the scrutiny of any Troll's eye. They had constructed underground ponds with ground water for bathing and drinking. Once a month they chose a group of 3 men to bravely enter the forest and forage for fruits, nuts and berries. It was a most dangerous task, but being familiar with the Troll's ways they nearly always escaped unseen and unharmed. Tonight 3 such Wimpet men Damien, Hector and Vincent were to become the latest group to be sent on this task.

The Nimbus fairies and Bjork were now deep within the realms of the forest. When they began to hear a loud groaning and rustling of branches. Jacor and Ryob looked at each other and Ryob whispered, " I think we may have an unwelcome visitor approaching, be on guard Jacor my friend". They proceeded ahead with caution, their senses in full capacity as they awaited the inevitable encounter. Anticipating the use of their bows, and looking at Nimrod for approval.

Nimrod whispered, " Don't fire upon them, there are not that many, we need not attract more. Remember Bjork's safety is in our hands."

An acrid smell began to fill their surroundings, and with one whiff they knew it was the rotting flesh smell of the Trolls. Ahead of them was a small clearing and they could see the awful beasts as they sat around a blazing fire. Their hideous features were quite apparent by firelight. They were so grotesque and disgusting. They appeared to be roasting one of their victim's upon a spit. They hastily applied the fish oil to Bjork's head and to theirs also. The combined scents were stomach-wrenching as they fought to keep from vomiting. Jeziah Nimrod and Mahew had also smelled and heard the Trolls and they too had applied the fish oil to their heads. They now stopped and hovered waiting for Bjork, Jacor and Ryob to catch up. When they were all gathered together, Nimrod spoke ever so softly, "We must think of a plan to distract these beasts so that we may continue on our journey."

Jeziah was deep in thought. After what seemed like hours but in reality were only minutes, he spoke. "This is the plan. We must wait for the Skinks to approach and then hang on to their underbellies with all our might as they scurry away from the Trolls. We will meet up together on the other side of the clearing."

CHAPTER 3

THE WIMPETS

They all waited breathlessly for the familiar sound of a Skink. Bjork and Jacor were the first two to experience hanging from the underbelly of a Skink. Oddly the Skinks didn't resist and seemed happy enough to oblige them. They had a peculiar wild scent about them and their skin was a strange rough wrinkled texture. It was difficult to get a grip into the flesh. But hang on for dear life they did until they were past the Troll clearing and on the edge of a valley. There was a pathway that wound through the valley with steep hills on both sides and borders of deep underbrush, it was a perfect resting place away from the Trolls. A place to regroup and make further plans. Ryob came along next accompanied by Nimrod. Both looked very amusing as they tried to gracefully dismount from the Skink, without losing their balance. Fairies never land on their backs, as it would break their wings, so when in danger of doing so they automatically go into a rotation and hover before they land carefully upon their feet.

Jeziah and Mahew were last to meet up with the rest. Together they decided that they must continue their journey above the ground and follow the winding path of the valley, which would lead them to the border of the Pastures of Lox. It was along this path that they encountered 3 strange looking wee people. They were covered in mud and leaves to camouflage themselves, and at first appearance had looked more like beasts than men. They startled Bjork's group and they hovered at a higher elevation carefully listening to their chatter. It was apparent they were speaking English dialect and seemed to be in a hurry. Damien the portly one of the bunch was extremely frightened, and kept mumbling to himself as he stumbled along the path." Lordy Lordy I do wish I were back home snug in my bed"

 Hector a thin sharp featured man spoke in disgust" Hush Damien you know we all must take turns gathering the food, it's only fair. If you don't be quiet the Trolls will surely hear us and we'll all be done for!" Vincent the youngest of the troop was neither thin nor fat, but was shorter than the others and quite content to be on this adventure. He was amused listening to Damien and Hector.

"Let's try to enjoy our night above ground, it may be a long while before we will do this again," he said smugly and sure of himself. He walked with a certain air of fearlessness.

Jacor took to the little fellow immediately and not thinking he said, "That's the attitude my lad, nothing to fear but fear itself I always say." The Wimpets stopped dead in their tracks, clearly puzzled from the sound of a strange voice. They couldn't see anything in the darkness and were deeply afraid that Jacor was an enemy laying in wait for them. Immediately Jacor knew what he had done and gracefully fluttered to the ground within view of the 3 Wimpets. They stood awestruck for they had heard tell of the fairy men, but had never laid eyes upon one. "Pardon me for my intrusion", Jacor said with true humility. "I couldn't help to admire the courage of your outspoken friend," he replied.

Hector spoke first" No harm done, although you did give us quite a start", he chuckled and extended his hand in friendship. "Excuse the mud and leaves we are wearing to protect us from the Trolls, it is a pleasure to make your acquaintance", he said. Soon the rest of the Bjork clan had introduced themselves one by one to the three Wimpet men. The Wimpets learned of Bjork's perilous journey and they vowed to show them safe passage through the underground city to the borders of Lox. In return Bjork and his group would help the Wimpets forage for their fruits and berries, safely above the ground and out of the Trolls reach. It was a fine idea and in no time with the extra help the Wimpets had gathered more than enough food, their sacks were overflowing. They began their way back to the entrance of the underground city. They were traveling quickly above ground. Bjork and Jacor, Ryob and Damien, Jeziah and Hector, Vincent and Mahew. All was going well, when along the path ahead they heard the familiar groaning and smelt the awful scent of Trolls. Now what would they do??????

They were carrying such heavy loads that it would take all their energy to hover for long. Bjork and Jacor decided to go on ahead of the group to investigate the situation. They courageously flew on along the path until around the bend they could faintly see the form of a Troll resting upon a stump. It was a female Troll and she was huge and ghastly hideous, she was crying a pitiful moan" Where are ye Bosha? , My poor dear wee one, come home to your Ma," she wailed. It seems her Troll child had become lost and she was in a deep panic. Little did they know that Bosha was the prince child of Dracor the Troll king. A terrible and bloodthirsty king that sent his fellow trolls out on patrol to capture and kill any strangers that crossed their paths.

Bjork and Jacor returned to tell the others. According to Hector the stump the Troll woman sat upon was the very entrance to their underground city. Jeziah, who had been listening intently, seized the moment to announce his newest idea. "If we find the Troll child and scare him he'll cry out for his Ma. She'll run off in the direction of his cries and we'll be able to sneak past and quickly enter the stump passage.

So it began their search for Bosha the Troll child. They flew out in all directions making a wide circle of the area, it was decided that whoever laid eyes upon the child first would take it upon themselves to scare it anyway that they could. A short time had elapsed when suddenly Ryob noticed a rustling in the underbrush, and upon closer view he could see the Troll child deep in slumber. It was strangely cute in a hideous sort of way its restless sleep had created the rustling as it tossed and turned. Quickly without haste he flew to it's side and frantically flapped his wings. He then coughed loudly three times; upon the third cough the Troll child awoke and began a fretful holler. Ryob ascended to a higher altitude to wait. The wailing of the Troll child could be heard far and wide. But even louder were the sounds of the Ma Troll calling its name "Bosha" and running through the underbrush. With no hesitation the Bjork group and their newfound Wimpet friends, after hearing the commotion flew to the entrance of the underground city. There on the side of the stump was a somewhat loose flap of bark. When the Wimpets pressed upon the top it fell wide open. There inside was a dark winding path leading down into the ground and in the far distance you could see a dim light. "Hurry my friends!" Hector cried, and in a flash all were safely inside and the door had been raised. He then slid a heavy piece of wood across the door through two secure wooden rings that held it in place. He smiled as he said" Come along for tonight we eat, drink and make merry, tomorrow we will show you safe passage to the Pasture of the Lox."

The other Wimpets and their families were very surprised indeed to greet their filthy fellowmen in the company of such strange and wonderful creatures. (What a sight they were indeed, they had too heard tales of fairy men, and often told stories to the Wimpet children of such, but none had ever laid eyes upon one for many, many centuries. The ones who had were long passed away. Also they were amazed at the sight of Bjork, Horks were just as rare in their land. The bounty of their forage was truly the best surprise of all. Never had they seen such a large harvest of fruits and nuts. They would not need to forage for quite some time. They could skip next year's trip altogether, for dried fruits and shelled nuts kept for a very long time in their large cool cellars. The 3 Wimpets excused themselves to clean up and prepare for the festivities. " Make yourselves at home," Hector called as he hurried along the winding path.

They took the extra time to explore the underground city. What a grand place it was. Little homes were cut into the face of the walls. In the center was a huge meeting place with hearths for cooking and benches for sitting. There were brightly lit torches that hung from the ceilings. More paths led to large storage rooms , libraries, hospital facilities and more. It would take forever to explore it fully. With no time to waste they returned to the meeting place to wait for the celebration to begin.

The Nimbus fairy men and Bjork were in for a rare treat. It was a lavish Wimpet feast, with jovial music playing from their homemade violins, and dancing. The single Wimpet women were very beautiful indeed and very graceful partners, and this along with their beautiful voices singing and the intoxicating Wimpet Wine made from the finest fermented fruits, gave the men much pleasure. It would indeed be a very pleasant diversion on their arduous journey. Tonight was just what they needed, rest, relaxation, good food and drink in good company. For tomorrow the journey would resume and once inside the Pastures of the Lox they would need fresh minds and all their strength and energy. For new perils awaited them and new adventures.

The evening was indeed a joyous occasion. The Bjork clan enjoyed themselves immensely. The food was delicious and the Wimpet people were a pleasant distraction from their tasks on hand. Ryob had as usual overindulged in spirits and was busy flirting with three young Wimpet beauties. But tomorrow would be here soon enough and so even though they normally would have celebrated back home into the wee hours of the morning, there celebrations were cut short tonight. Bjork graciously thanked his hosts for the wonderful evening and begged forgiveness for having to retire so soon. In the midst of their celebrations the Bjork clan hadn't paid too much attention to an old withered Wimpet figure that sat huddled in the corner watching but not participating in the festivities. But now Hector stepped forward and said," my dear new friends you mustn't retire without first meeting the eldest and wisest Wimpet of all, my father Methezdah". With the mention of his name the frail figure rose and Bjork was amazed at how much he resembled the Nimrod fairy's Nebuccanezzar. The older Wimpet bowed and waved his hand in a come forward gesture.

Bjork and his clan approached the wise Wimpet full of curiosity as he slowly and carefully spoke in his worn and raspy voice, "It is with utmost pleasure that I Methezdah make your acquaintances. My father Ramrod and his before him had traveled above the ground and had met the likes of both your peoples. I am surprised to find that I have lived long enough to see that the stories he told me of your appearances were quite accurate. This is indeed a pleasure that I never dreamed of in my lifetime. I must return the favor for the joy you have given me by placing the Wimpet blessing upon you all before you leave tomorrow on your fateful journey. Bring me the anointing robes and the oils and my staff Hector," he cried.

The garments of spun gold and the sweet smelling oils were soon before them also there was a strange oddly carved wooden staff that resembled a snake. When Methezdah wrapped the robes about him and anointed the heads of the Bjork clan the wooden staff was placed into his hand. In truly amazing fashion it began to writhe and shake and take on the form of a real snake as Methezdah muttered, 'Withalda Withalda anointa testa!" and pointed the staff directly at each one of the Bjork clan. He repeated his incantation four times and then strangely passed the oil chalice, which had now become a strange tasting wine. They all took a drink and immediately they felt an odd peacefulness come over them. When the last had drank Methezdah spoke once more," Sleep well my dear new friends, we shall rejoice upon your victorious return from Lox."

"Come now friends," spoke Hector, ""Damien will show you your lodging quarters for the night. I will see you all bright and early tomorrow." So off they went through the winding passages and down the dim lit stairwells until they were led into a large chamber with many separate rooms, each had there own comfortable bed, and all the comforts of home. According to Bjork's timepiece it was well after midnight. Hector had agreed to awaken early and summons the clan for their tour through the Wimpet Township. Being a Wimpet he was under no urgency in his simple lifestyle, and simply slept when he was tired and rose when he felt like it. They had no need to know the time of day. Bjork's timepiece had amused him and so the fact that other living creatures could be prisoners of time, forced to wake, eat and sleep according to its passage. How strange he thought to be summoned awake and live one's life on a set schedule according to the time of day. Therefore he had asked Bjork to wake him in the morning. Bjork blew out his candle and laid himself upon the small comfortable wooden bed, stretched his legs, yawned and rubbed his weary eyelids. In no time at all he was sound asleep. Up and down the winding paths could be heard the chorus of many Wimpets snoring in unison. Bjork's snoring soon fell right in sync with the others.

Bjork awoke with a start; he fumbled for a match in his pocket to light his bedside candle. Soon his chamber was filled with the dancing glow from its bright-lit wick. It flickered gently as he tried to adjust his eyes. Then he glanced at his timepiece that was set upon the table near the burning candle. It read 6 o'clock. He arose from his bed. How quiet it was, he could still hear the chorus of snoring and once in awhile an occasional cough, or clearing of a throat. He stood up and grabbed the candle by it's holder and started winding his way down the path, sticking his head into each room of his clan and beseeching them to come out "We must make haste my friend, he would cheerfully call," at each doorway. He received a pleasant reply from each fairy man. Being as they only rest and don't sleep, they are never grumpy even in the wee hours of the morning. Soon Bjork came to Hector's doorway." Hector my friend it is I Bjork, he whispered, it is time to give us our grand tour, arise my new friend".

"Wha---t a sleepy Hector replied, is it already time? He yawned deeply and said, "very well my friends I will be right with you." Soon the flicker of his candle could be seen, through the crack of his door, as he shuffled around his room getting dressed. In moments he stepped outside with his candle in hand. All the Wimpet folk wore the same attire. Shirts woven from the valley grasses and short pants to match. In the winter months they wore moleskin jackets and rat fur hats, and slippers.

Hector spoke in a rather sleepy yet cheerful voice, "Morning my friends, let us begin the tour, it'll take the better half of the day to reach the end of these tunnels." They each fell in to step behind him and as they traveled along the winding paths Hector would stop at each room and explain its function. There were so many marvelous rooms, and each was set aside for one special activity. There were the bathrooms, a very creative use of the hot springs, which bubbled up from the earthen floor, feeding into a deep channel that wound down to the huge carved out bathing pools.

Wimpets were a social group and they did everything in complete harmony with their kin. Evenings were spent in community baths. Where many a Wimpet voice would be raised in song. There was neither modesty nor humility in their simple culture. Nudity was quite acceptable. Other rooms were set aside for the daily washing of clothing, and there were rooms for clothes weaving, rooms for book reading, rooms for schooling, rooms for cooking, rooms for resting, rooms for everything. It was truly an underground world in itself. They had been winding their way through the tunnels now for sometime and had grown very hungry when Hector spoke," My friends up around the bend is the food cellar, let us rest awhile and partake of some nuts and nectar." The cellar was huge and there were tremendously large clay vats filled to the brim with every sort of nut and berry. Other huge clay urns were spilling over with delicious Wimpet nectar. Some of the aged nectar was used for special occasions and too much would soon lead to a drunken stupor. It was the unfermented that Hector and Bjork's clan drank. Sweet and good but harmless, there would be time to drink the aged nectar when they returned to celebrate their victory. They ate their fill and filled their pockets with nuts and their wine skins with nectar for the trip.

The Wimpets had proven to be a valuable deterrence from their quest. They would always remain friends to Bjork and the Nimbus fairy men.
They continued their tour through the winding caves and darkened passages, the stalactites and their dripping sounds echoed around them as they began slowly to ascend. The path was rising steady now. They no longer could hear the voices of the Wimpets. They were rising ever higher and higher. It was very tiring to keep up the pace and Bjork leaned against the wall of the path and asked in short breaths," Hector how much further is it? I feel my lungs will burst if I have to climb any further."

 Hector replied," See there around the bend that shaft of light? The end is near that shaft." Wearily Bjork pushed away from the wall and continued the climb. When they had turned the bend the light was much brighter and their eyes had difficulty at first adjusting to the change. Bjork squinted through his teary eyes, and looking closer he noticed the light was coming from what appeared to be a door, a door made of rock that was wedged tightly in place. The light was streaming from the cracks around it. Even if all of the fairy men Bjork and Hector tried with all their might, they would never dislodge this huge rock from its place, Bjork thought.

"Is there a way to remove the rock, Hector?" he said with a slight nudge and a look of disbelief.

Hector replied, "Aye there is, it's an old spell of my Father Methezdah that hasn't been used in a long, long time. I was hoping I would remember it by the time we reached here," he scratched his chin in deep thought as he spoke. I used it myself many years ago, "I'll try my very best", he said as his face deeply blushed with embarrassment." Let's see it started with Rock of safety, Rock of might, and then I think remove thyself and then I can't remember the rest. He appeared very nervous and anxious and was truly trying hard to remember the last three words. He tried many times," Remove thyself expose the light, remove thyself and hear my plight, remove thyself" ...Finally he stopped totally worn out and thoroughly ashamed and sat hardly upon the ground. "Forgive me my friends I neglected to ask my Father last night due to my pride, I was so sure that I would remember, forgive this old Wimpet and his foolish vanity!"

At that moment Mahew who had been quietly resting came forward, "Bjork I believe I can be of service here, I have devised a plan."

"By all means my fairy friend please do try" Bjork said as he extended his hand outward toward the foreboding rock. Mahew reached carefully inside the folds of his fairy garment and soon produced his drawing stick. He raised his wings in a triumphant gesture as he approached the huge barrier. In a flash he drew the perfect picture of an open door upon it, and just as magically it came to life. The land of Lox was before them, they could see the trees, hear the birds, feel the gentle breeze, and the sun's warmth as they stepped through the magical door. Mahew called back to Hector, "Here erase it as soon as we have all stepped through", as he tossed him a dry cloth. Hector grabbed the cloth and began to erase the door as Mahew disappeared from view. He could hear their voices growing fainter. As the door was completely erased he thought he heard a distinct growl. Then he stood back in silence looking at the solid rock where once an open door had been. This had been a very eventful couple of days with his odd new friends. The Hork Bjork and his entourage of mysterious Nimbus fairies now seemed almost like a dream. Hector yawned, he felt suddenly quite tired as he turned with his lantern and began the long walk back. I believe I will retire for a nap upon my return he thought.

"Return soon my friends, he called", but he only heard an echo of his voice.

CHAPTER FOUR

THE LAND OF LOX

Bjork looked over his shoulder just in time to see Mahew stepping through the door. The sun was brightly shining and he could smell the sweet scent of pollen in the air. The trees and flowers were all dripping with sparkling dewdrops. It gave them the appearance of being draped in jewels. He had never, (even in his own flowering gardens at home), seen such rare beauty as this. There were flowers of all shapes and sizes bursting with every color imaginable. It was strange to think what odd companions these glorious flowers made with the Hideous Lox beasts. How they shared this same habitat in complete harmony was absurd. He was bending over to smell the scent of an extremely large wildflower, when he first heard the deep growls. Instantly Jacor appeared to swoop him safely off his feet. The others too had flown to higher ground to spy on the origin of these growls. They were quite far up a lofty cliff sitting in the shadows peering down upon the low lands. It was hard to see through all the trees, plants and flowers. They didn't dare to make a sound. It seemed to be getting a little closer and louder now. Bjork shook off a shiver and leaned forward a bit, trying to get a better view. Then the plants rustled right beneath them and just the tip of the fierce wagging tail could be seen rising out from amidst the flowers. "A Lox," he whispered to himself.

They all remained still as they waited and watched the beast. It continued to growl and then it snorted and turned its large head. They immediately fell upon their bellies in silence as the beast parted the tall leaves and stepped into a small clearing below them. Its head was massive with huge ox like horns and a lion's mane. The chest was a mass of hard muscle as well as the legs and the feet were cloven. The tail looked much like a lion's, and was now held up in proud defiance. What was it after, they wondered. They kept lying flat in the shadows as they waited for their question to be answered. It once again let out a huge growl and as it's lips parted it showed it's awful fangs. It began to claw at the ground and it's growl turned more into a strange deep moaning.

In all the commotion the clan didn't notice another growl in the distance that was growing louder now.

Bjork felt goosebumps rise upon his flesh. In terrible fear now, he realized another Lox would soon be joining the other. Would even more appear?? His mind raced as he tried to think a way out of this dilemma.

Then the growls became so loud that Bjork thought he couldn't stand to hear them anymore. He shut his eyes in pure terror. Such terrible sounds they made, horribly awful sounds he thought. It was much worse than   the sounds he heard in his worst nightmares. He forced himself to open one eye and as he did, he saw the leaves part once again and into the clearing stepped another Lox. This one was of smaller stature, it didn't have horns, and wore a longer mane. It appeared to be either an offspring or female of the species.

By the other Lox's reaction it was soon apparent that it was indeed a female. Within moments a rather noisy mating ritual began. The male Lox would approach the female and she would playfully swat at him with her claws and hiss. The male grew angrier and much louder, growling and snorting at her.

It was at this time that Bjork's clan decided to make their escape. "Those two are so pre-occupied that they won't notice us at all," Nimrod said. With that Jacor grabbed Bjork and off they all flew above the cliff and down the other side into a lush green pasture. They remained at flight looking for signs of more Lox and for the greatly sought after Juju berry bushes. Bjork knew he had come very far and that he was so close to obtaining the cure for his lovely Naomi. But he felt an eerie sense of doom and tried to shake it off.

 The sun was getting lower now and there was an uncanny quiet to the land. The sunset was such an amazing bright orange so beautiful and reminiscent of days gone by in the land of the Horks. Bjork's mind started to wander off peacefully to another place and another time (a time of youth and youthful pleasures.) Such was the feeling of contentment that came as the sun bid its final goodbye for the day. Such was the cheerful calling of the mother Horks as each reminded their young children that it was time to return home for the evening supper. Such an evening was this, that for a moment he forgot where he was. When all of a sudden Jacor was yanking on his arm and calling in a very persistent voice. "Bjork, Bjork dear fellow we've found the JUJU berry bushes, we must hurry before night falls." Instantly he remembered his dear Naomi and sprang into action.

"Yes Jacor we must quickly fill our empty bags and find shelter for the night." With the help of his faithful companions, each in turn gathering the JUJU berries; their bags were filled in no time. Bjork synched the bags closed and let go a deep sigh of relief. They then began to search for a safe area to spend the night.

It was Jeziah who spoke then. "I know you are pretty much worn out from the day Bjork, but nimbus fairies travel well at night, we need not rest nor tarry in this dangerous land. I believe it is best if we use the cover of darkness as our cloak and soar high above ground until we reach the point of return. The LOX do their hunting at night and if we fly quickly enough and shield you they won't be able to catch your scent. You will have plenty of time for rest when we enter the Wimpet's underground city."

Bjork was too tired to argue and he knew in his heart that Jeziah was right. So he nodded his head in agreement and they began their flight home. They had only been flying for a few minutes when they all heard the terrible commotion. Such terrible screams that sounded almost human. Only the mighty roar of the Lox and the sound of them wrestling upon the ground could compete with the screams. It was then that they saw them, a group of small Gnomes, it appeared to be a family of 5. Three wee ones and two adult. They were hiding beneath the leaves of a large fern, shaking, and trembling in fear. It was the littlest of these that had been screaming, but now all were silent at their parent's command. We heard the older male one speak," Hush my children, we must not let the Lox find us, surely it will be the death of us all", as he raised his forefinger to his lips. Apparently the Lox were fighting amongst themselves over some poor beast that had fallen prey to them. They hadn't noticed the screams of the wee ones.

 Nimrod spoke with authority, "Even now I hear my sister Naomi calling for the cure that we possess, yet in my heart I know I can't leave these Gnomes to fend for themselves. Being an elder Nimbus and heir to the throne, it is my responsibility to protect the weaker creatures of this world. Have patience my friend Bjork", he said as he placed his hand upon Bjork's shoulder." My comrades let us rescue this wee family together." So while the Lox continued to fight over the spoils, the Nimbus fairy clan swiftly flew to the Gnomes rescue. They were startled at first by the fairy's presence, and Jacor had to remind the wee ones not to speak. Soon it was all explained how the Gnomes had been out enjoying the wonderful sunset and collecting pine nuts. Their offspring had wanted to tarry against the Father Gnomes better judgment. Nonetheless he had agreed to stay for just a while longer. They began their journey back to their home as the sun was making its last appearance near the horizon.

It seems they lived in the side of a green hill, their door was a mole hole, and this large mole in return for feeding it protected them, it lived mainly on a large diet of earthworms. The small Gnomes loved to dig in the dirt outside the hole and catch the wiggly worms, so they were allowed to do so under the watchful protection of the mole, which stood guard nearby. It was a very strange arrangement, which worked out well for all involved. The Lox never bothered the moles, so they never knew of the Gnome's existence.

 The Gnomes were coming near to the edge of the Lox forest where it led to the green pastures of the JUJU berry, a Gnome delicacy, when they came upon the fighting Lox. They were all too happy for the protection of the Nimbus fairies. The Father Gnome a rather stout fellow with a large pointed hat, and a nose to match, stepped forward and extended his hand in a gesture of friendship." Pleased ta meet ye, name's Higgins," he grumbled, and this be my fine wifey here Rosey and our two youngins Tiff and Taff, "Rosey was the perfect name for this small frame female Gnome, her cheeks were indeed round and rosy pink in color. She wore her hair upon her head in bun fashion and had a very full round figure. Her eyes sparkled blue as she smiled and said, "I insist that once we reach home you stay on for a little supper and some fresh JUJU berry tarts." Bjork's stomach growled a hungry reply; he indeed could use a little bite to eat. So all agreed upon it as each fairy took hold of the Gnomes one by one and Bjork and they flew off in the direction of the

Gnome's hillside home. When they reached the wooden door, Higgins threw it open and said," Welcome my friends, do make yourselves at home.
 It was beautiful inside; there were large drawings on the walls of forest scenes. Carefully carved wooden chairs and tables. Beautiful wooden desks and shelves with many hand-carved wooden statues. The Gnomes were skilled woodcrafters and their sculptures were very life-like and three-dimensional. Bjork was appreciating the fine workmanship of a Lox beast that was sitting on the shelf, when Rosey called, " Supper is ready, come now, let's eat."
 What a feast it was indeed, some of the finest nuts, wild yams and berries of the forest. Washed down with a sweet fermented honey nectar and finished off with a delicious Juju berry tart. Bjork wiped away the crumbs from his lips and sighed in contentment. Higgins was happy to have strangers to talk to. It had been a long time since he had been able to practice his social skills. He sat at the head of the table and spoke with a slow serious tone. " Excuse me friends, my manners may be a little rusty," he said. "It's been a long time since I've entertained company." "The last time I believe was about 5 years ago when I met the acquaintance of Syncore the Sailor. He was searching for a river that was believed to have run straight through the continent and out to the Eastern sea. He spoke of many places near and far where he had traveled. He was a very large and muscular sort, with a stubbly growth of blonde hair upon his chin, and a dark complexion. His face bore the tan of a seaman, and his laughter was deep and contagious. All he carried with him was a pack that he slung over his shoulder, which contained his pipe and tobacco, a flask of some curious ale, a compass and many rolled up maps .He

stayed on for a few days, and then mysteriously disappeared, never to be seen or heard from again." Higgins blushed, "But forgive my rudeness, please tell me all about yourselves," he said.

Bjork proceeded to tell him the story of Naomi and the JuJu berry cure. Higgins rested his chin in his hands and listened quite contently to every word. It was growing very late when they bid their Gnome friends a fine farewell and flew off into the night, in search of the doorway to the Wimpet City.

CHAPTER FIVE

HOMEWARD BOUND

It seemed as if they were flying in circles, everything looked the same. How would they find the magical doorway? Bjork was growing frustrated and worried about the impending dawn. If they were spotted in the daylight the Lox would put up a mighty chase. He felt too weary from lack of sleep to survive one of their attacks. He remembered Methezdah's blessing and silently prayed that it would lead them in the right direction. It was at that moment when he heard a strange sound as of the wind whistling through tall trees, and he turned in its direction. There before his eyes he saw a strange bluish fog moving slowly upon the ground, traveling towards them. He looked at Nimrod, Jacor, Jeziah, Mahew, and Ryob for their reaction. They too were puzzled by it's appearance. It drew within reach of them as they all stood frozen, taken in by it's spell. Then it began to fade and a shape began to appear, not clearly recognizable at first. Then a familiarity came with the shape as it become sharper and clearer until at last there stood old Methezdah himself.

He looked upon Bjork's startled face and smiled, "Bjork I believe you have summoned me for some purpose, (as he cleared his throat A-hem), and paused waiting for Bjork's reply. "Oh yes sir, Oh yes, indeed I did, it seems we are lost and can't find our way back to Wimpet City," Bjork blushed in embarrassment. "Well, well, hmm," Methezdah said as he stroked his long pointed beard," I believe it's right over there!" as he swung his arm out straight and pointed his finger. They all stood in awe as they watched the doorway appear upon the side of a hill a few yards away. They could even see the flickering of torchlight from the passages that were beyond its entrance. "Hurry make haste before sunlight, "Jacor cried as he grabbed Bjork and they all flew quickly to the entrance. Bjork looked over his shoulder and felt a strange chill, and shuddered as they quickly flew inside and the doorway instantly sealed up! Where was Methezdah he wondered?

They began their way back through the winding passages, anxious to see their old friend Hector again, and to tell him of their fortune. I must ask him about Methezdah he said to himself. The torchlight led them through the familiar pathways until they reached the large banquet room. Here they sat and waited for the Wimpets to awaken and begin their new day. Bjork had grown so weary, and feeling very safe now he laid his head down upon the table and soon fell fast asleep. He slept and dreamt of his youth and of beautiful Naomi.

A few hours had passed when he was awoken by the gently shaking of his friend Hector. "Bjork, Bjork, my friend I'm so pleased to see that all is well with you." "Come I will show you to a room where you may sleep in comfort," he said. Bjork was too tired to argue, as he stumbled down the path behind Hector he said, "Hector I mustn't forget to thank Methezdah for his help last night." "Where might he be found?" Hector looked as if he had seen a ghost, "Methezdah?? Last night??? "Bjork that is impossible, My Father Methezdah died last week of old age." He was buried two days ago."

""I'm so sorry to hear this news, my condolences to you and yours Hector," Bjork replied. Hector sadly grabbed Bjork's shoulder, squeezed it and said, ""I've expected this for sometime now, he will be greatly missed.""

Bjork tossed and turned fretfully as he slept. Visions of Methezdah filled his head. He could hear Naomi's shallow breathing, as she laid waiting for the Juju berry cure. He awoke drenched in a cold sweat and sat shivering on the edge of his bed. Unable to sleep anymore, he rose, dressed and lit the candle sitting by his bed. He could hear the patterned breathing of the Wimpet's as they slept, some of them snoring almost in harmony. The sound filled his chamber and made him long for home and for sleep in his own comfortable bed. He wrapped the tattered edges of his green gown around his frail shoulders and sighed. How I wish its powers could transport me there now he thought. But he knew too well its powers of transportation were limited to Hork Land. Grabbing the candle he began his walk back into the banquet room. He felt a strange chill up his spine as if he was being watched and followed as he made his way slowly through the winding passages. He kept a careful quick pace and glanced on occasion over his shoulder, never seeing a sign of what was apparently following behind. It gave him a queer eerie feeling, yet he wasn't at all frightened. It was almost as if the follower was an old and dear friend. When he turned the corner and the banquet room lay straight ahead, he felt as if it had given up chase. He shrugged it off as simple imagination, a trick his weary mind was playing on him perhaps.

Once inside the banquet room, he found a cozy nook and settled in to wait for his friend Hector and the other Wimpets to awaken and begin their morning rituals. There on the seat beside him he felt something large and fairly heavy, he held his candle nearer and upon inspection he read on its cover "Tales of the Wimpet King". Hmm, he thought that's odd, I have never heard mention of a Wimpet king before. The book was worn and it's corners were tattered from many a curious readers touch. He opened the cover and read, "To my dear friend Bjork, May he read this book and believe in miracles! Yours Respectfully, Methezdah.

How had he known that Bjork would choose this bench to sit upon? The thought was very intriguing indeed. He laid the hefty volume upon the tabletop and sat staring in amazement as he thought of Methezdah's recent passing. Believe in miracles he thought, my dear friend Methezdah, thanks to you I have been witness to them. He knew he would treasure this gift for the rest of the days of his life. It would be proudly read and displayed upon his mantle for all Horks to see. He would pass it on in death to the worthiest Hork he could find. He did wonder though how he would carry it back; it was so large and heavy.

The Wimpets slowly began to fill the banquet area, each with their own specific chore. He couldn't wait until the morning meal was served, he suddenly felt ravenous, as if he hadn't eaten in days. The smell of the hot porridge had whetted his appetite. What a joy the hot grog was, as a large steaming mug was placed before him.

He would hate to leave this peaceful place. But he knew he must make haste to return to Naomi. Her very existence depending upon him, he couldn't let her and the Nimbus fairies down. So when Hector appeared in the doorway he quickly motioned to him to come and join him. Soon they were chatting like old friends as Bjork told his tale of the land of Lox, and his Gnome encounters. Hector was speechless as he hung on every word. "Ah to be so blessed as to travel and have adventures as these, it makes my heart grow envious, he said, with a faraway look in his eyes. I see you have found the gift My Father Methezdah left for you. He left explicit orders that it not be disturbed from its resting place, and that no one was to speak a word of it, not even us Wimpets to each other. He said that you would be more convinced if you found it yourself. Bjork smiled knowingly and said, " I am truly convinced, and I am sure this book will keep this old Hork warm on many a cold night. I look forward to a long a rewarding relationship with this very special

gift." "Ah that reminds me," Hector said. " My Father instructed me to give you this tote sack to carry the book in." He produced a rather small sack. "But it will never fit in that", Bjork said as he turned to look at the book.
He couldn't believe his eyes for there in its place sat the same identical book, only this one was 1/4 of the size and weight. He grinned sheepishly and placed it in the sack." I should have known that Methezdah would think of everything, even how I would carry his gift home," he said.

He rose and stood to warmly embrace his friend Hector, and gave a nod to the Nimbus fairy men. " It deeply saddens me to bid you farewell, but I must be on my way. I will never forget your kindness and if I ever pass this way again I will be sure to drop in for a spell. " "May you all be truly blessed with peace and happiness." He bowed graciously, then gathered his book and turned to see if Nimrod and his men had retrieved the Juju berries. Although small in size the fairymen were as strong as any human man. Each had their synched sack carefully in tow as they waited for Bjork to offer his goodbyes.

It was a familiar path they took now as Hector led them through the winding passages upward toward the stump, that served as their entrance door. Bjork wondered what perils they would find as they entered once again into the Land of the Trolls. He felt a strange flow of adrenalin rushing through his veins, a reminder of his youth. He felt a sense of urgency and a strength within himself that would let nothing else stand in the way of his returning to Naomi's side. He could picture giving her the cure and her breathing, growing stronger, her beautiful eyes opening..............

In no time at all they were at the top of the passage and a faint ray of light could be seen through the edges of the stump's trap door. It was daylight so they must prepare for the worst. "Nimrod, do we have anymore of that fish oil left? Bjork asked. "Yes, I have a vial left, it should be enough to cover your scent, Nimrod said". He produced it from a pocket in his vest that was hidden beneath a wing. Bjork wasted no time covering his head with the awful smelling oil. "Blessings go with you all", Hector said as he watched them go through the door, and then hastily pulled it shut. He wiped a tear from his cheek knowing that he would not live to see these friends again. Then his shoulders drooped in sorrow as he slowly walked down the passage, leading back to his Wimpet family.

Bjork cautiously peered into the foliage listening intently for any signs of the Trolls. His stomach was turning from the acrid scent of fish oil. He felt strangely tired even after his long night's sleep. The Nimbus fairies were quite busy trying to carry their juju berries, all of their senses alert for any signs of danger. It would be long before the sun set, and they wouldn't take flight until necessary. They needed to preserve their strength for the harsh environment of Endure.
They had traveled some time now without any incident and were becoming to have a false sense of security, when the repulsive scent came wafting along through the breeze and filled their minds with instant terror. Trolls! There were many trolls, from the smell. Jacor wasted no time in grabbing Bjork and took flight

to a high branch of a tall old oak tree. He signaled to the others to join him for a quick assessment of their situation and hopefully an idea of how to reach safe harbor. As they sat upon the branches they could now clearly see and unfortunately smell, a large group of Trolls (perhaps 5 or more), which were headed in their direction.

Jacor spoke courageously " I will protect us, I've slain many of these ghastly Trolls, (as he reached for his bow and arrows.) It was Bjork that sadly shook his head and replied, "Tis true you have my dear friend, but I fear even you are no match for this large group. I must refuse your kind offer. I feel responsible for the dangerous situation I have put us all in. I can't stand idle and allow you to fight alone for my benefit." Just then they noticed another larger group of about the same size coming from another direction towards them. Jeziah was deep in thought, he finally spoke," Jacor I must agree with Bjork my friend , even you cannot possibly stave off all of these," as he gestured toward the trolls with his outstretched hands. Then he pointed at Bjork's gown and spoke.

"Bjork the green gown that Naomi gave you, does it not have special powers?" Bjork frowned and sighed as he spoke." Yes it does but my memory fails me as to which spell to recite for them." If I use the wrong spell it would be disastrous for us all." There are some to conjure up beasts, some for lightening and thunder, and one that is for transformation," he scratched his chin as he pondered further." Naomi did give me a copy of the instruction for fairy spells, but it's home sitting upon a shelf in my library." I should have known to bring it with me, but I didn't want it to fall into the wrong hands." "Oh Nebuccaneezer my friend I wish you were here now", he sighed.

The Trolls were quickly approaching now and they could do nothing but sit helplessly upon their branches high above the Troll's heads. "I hope they don't look up and see us, Nimrod said," they've been known to clear trees very fast with their strong arms and mighty axes." Bjork closed his eyes in fear. It was just then that he felt a familiar tapping upon his shoulder and as he opened his eyes and rubbed them in disbelief there sat before him Nebuccaneezer himself. He was straddling the branches carefully when he reached his hand inside his robe and removed his magic wand. How welcome was his old wizen face, as he spoke, "I heard your plea Bjork and came as quickly as possible." "Hmm, he said looking down in the direction of the trolls." I see you're in imminent danger, how can I be of service?" "Shall I conjure up a large Cyclops to slay them all?"

"Nay I think I would have more pleasure in witnessing the powers of your gown." Once again he reached inside his pocket and this time his hand came out clutching the copy of fairy spells that Bjork had needed.

"This is your adventure my old dear friend, he said, I will not rob you of the glory of defeating your enemies yourself."

" But how did you know what I needed?" Bjork asked. Nebuccaneezer gave a wink and vanished into thin air. Nothing was left not even a leaf turned to show that he had been there.

 The Trolls were directly underneath as Bjork thumbed through the pages until he found the spell for transformation. "Yes I believe this will suit us just fine," he smiled as he spoke. "Nimbus que nimbus quo turn this gown into a TROLL!" Instantly he was transformed into a large ghastly hairy smelly Troll. He barely fit upon the branches as he grabbed each fairy and their juju berries and tucked them beneath his smelly shirt. "Now we'll simply walk right out of here, he said triumphantly. He handed Nimrod who was riding in his upper pocket the copy of spells. And said "Whatever you do don't lose these, or I'll never be able to undo the spell.

He swung down to the ground just in time to meet head-on with the Troll group. They grunted a greeting and he grunted back .He turned away and began taking long strides. Being this size has its advantages he thought I should reach the land of Endure in half the time. Nebuccaneezer was right, it did feel grand to get oneself out of a predicament. Bjork hadn't felt so proud and sure of himself in a very, very long time.

Meanwhile back in the Nimbus fairy meadow Caliope paced anxiously. He watched the Nimbus fairy women attending to Naomi. They wiped the sweat from her brow as she moaned and tossed and turned in her sleep. How lonely he would be if he lost her. But NO! He mustn't even think such terrible things." Nimrod and Bjork will succeed," he muttered. (Afraid that the other fairies would hear him.) They mustn't think I've lost faith he thought. He closed his eyes and uttered a fairy prayer and walked back toward where Naoimi lies. He sat down next to her to keep watch until Nimrod and Bjork's return.

CHAPTER SIX

ALMOST HOME

It was getting rather late as Bjork finally reached the
border of Endure. The sun was setting in the sky, and
he could smell the arid scent of a land, which had not
seen rain for many long years. It had a strange dusty
odor that clung heavily to his nostrils as he looked
wearily around for a place to rest. Off to the distance
he could see what appeared to be a very ancient
rotting tree stump. He headed in that direction as he
released his captive fairy men from their hiding places.
"Whew!" Nimrod said,' It was beginning to get quite
stuffy in there", as he winked at Bjork. "I must rest for
a bit now, and then I will attempt to undo this spell,
Bjork muttered. They all laughed. It was very strange
to see such a large ugly beast that sounded just like
their dear friend Bjork. Bjork sat down upon the stump
and grabbed a flask from his robe. The cool water
parched his dry throat, and he began to feel more at
ease. They were on the last legs of their journey now.
As far as he knew there were no more dangers to lie
ahead. Everyone was very sure that nothing could
survive in such a desolate place as this. He slid from the
stump to the ground beneath and sat leaning back
against it, now completely relaxed. "Nimrod hand me
the spell book, I can't bare the smell of myself any
longer ", he chuckled, and reached out his large Troll
hand. Nimrod quickly obliged and soon Bjork was
standing and chanting, Nimbus quo Nimbus Que
Troll now my green gown be. Instantly he was back to

himself standing in his green gown, perhaps a little more weary, but no harm done.

"We can travel quite well here after dark, it will be cooler, let us rest awhile longer", he said. With that Bjork stood and pointed to what looked like a cave on the side of a tall hill. That looks like a place where I might sleep for a bit," as he stretched and yawned," we'll soon be back in the Nimbus meadow, I won't sleep long." It looked harmless enough, so they agreed and soon they were all deep inside. It was cool and dark, and they could hear the echo of Bjork's footsteps as he moved cautiously through the cave. He found a spot where the ground was smooth and free of rocks. He lay down curled up on his side and soon was fast asleep. They could hear his snores echoing from the chamber walls. This was a comforting sound to them all, as they had all grown rather fond of Bjork. Each fairy man stretched out for a rest and sat their Juju berries down. Bjork was right; a rest would be nice they agreed. They envied Bjork the ability to sleep, something they had never done in all their years. But fairies had too many enemies and had to be wary at all times. The evil creatures were jealous of the peaceful natured fairies and the powers they possessed. Some wished them death and other captivity. They could never let their guard down lest they become something's dinner, or pet.

They were resting quite peacefully, when all of a sudden they heard a strange hissing sound. It was approaching them from deep inside the cave. It echoed off the walls as they sat and waited, wondering what could possible live here. Bjork awoke with a startle and sat up, "What is that strange noise I hear?" he asked.

He shuddered when he felt the hot breath upon his back, and pleaded
in stutters," Please whatever you are, I intend you no harm, forgive my intrusion, I didn't realize...........Jacor wasted no time in appearing by Bjork's side. He stood there in defiance with his bow drawn and his arrow pointed at the direction of the hissing. It was much too dark to make out what exactly it was.

 Fairies have the ability to faintly glow when angered, and this could be a dangerous situation for Jacor. Although he could not see the hissing creature, it was surely able to see him, just as clearly as Bjork could. "I won't let you talk me out of protecting you now," Jacor said. Bjork was very grateful to have such a good marksman traveling with him. The hissing beast grew louder as Jacor let go of his bowstrings and his arrow made its entrance into it's flesh. He repeated his attack until his quiver was empty and the hissing grew fainter and fainter, and only the sounds of their beating hearts was left.

Bjork sat in silence afraid to move lest there be more creatures that dwelt in this cave. "Let's leave this dreadful place he whispered." He rose and was about to leave when he heard a strange echo of uneven footsteps. He turned to Nimrod and said, "Hurry! and started to run in what he thought was the direction that he had come. But the cave was a maze of winding, twisted and turning paths and now he was running even deeper into its dark abode. The Nimbus fairies were in hot pursuit. "Bjork! Bjork! Ryob called," You're going the wrong way." Bjork ran as if he had seen death look him in the face, he couldn't hear anything but the sound of his own frightened footsteps. He turned a corner and ran smack into something large, it knocked him off his feet and he found himself frightened, alone , hurt and sitting in the dark. Then he heard it; it appeared to be laughing at him. Yes it was the distinct sound of very hearty laughter. Then he heard the striking of a match, as the chamber came to light from the bright glowing torch that the laughing creature held. There before him stood a strange looking dwarf, covered in armor. It looked as though his armor was made from the skin of reptiles. He wore a helmet and carried a crude made ax (hewn from wood with a blade of sharp stone.) "Be not in fear stranger," he spoke." My name is Morgan, I be of the Cavedweller clan." "You have saved me the trouble of slaying that awful Sandserpent." "I don't get visitors here very often. We rarely leave the cave. I have heard tell of Nimbus fairy folks, and Horks, there are ancient pictures drawn on the inner chamber walls of your kind. But this is the first time I've seen either in the flesh. It's so grand to have company, let me show you around. I'd love to treat you to a Cavedweller feast, come meet the clan, "he spoke rapidly, excitedly and pointed in friendly fashion with his torch in the direction they would go.

Bjork was amused, this journey has been full of surprises he thought. He smiled and spoke" Morgan let me introduce myself, "I'm Bjork the Hork and these are my Nimbus fairy friends, Nimrod, Jacor, Ryob, Mahew, and Jeziah. We accept your gracious hospitality. You must tell me all about yourselves. I want to know everything."
"Come then my guests the evening is young", Morgan said with a grin. In the torch light Bjork could see he had a full rather boyish face with long bushy eyebrows

and a small bushy mustache and beard. His cheeks were round and his nose a little turned up on the end. He had long pointy ears that poked up from the brim of his reptile helmet. His boots were laced high and they appeared to be made from the same type of reptile skin as his armor. Indeed he was a strange yet friendly little fellow, Bjork thought as they followed him deeper into the cave. The path wound round and down and their only light was the glow of Morgan's torch. The fairies flew along close behind appearing to be a parade of faint lights that danced on the cave walls behind him. Deeper and deeper they went, with only the sound of Bjork and Morgan's footsteps. Then off in the distance Bjork could faintly hear the sounds of music, and children at play. Their voices grew louder as they continued ahead through the passages, until they wound down around a corner and came upon a steep long path that spiraled downward. The steps were carved in the stone beneath his feet and carefully spaced apart, to give the cave dwellers (who had small strides) a safe staircase to climb. As they neared the bottom step the music was now much louder, and as Bjork looked to his left he could see another passage brightly lit by torches that hung suspended from the walls. (The path, which Morgan now followed). Bjork could now smell a delicious scent of something unfamiliar cooking. He hurried along behind until the passage came to an open room filled with cave dwellers at play. Young and old were singing , dancing and playing music. The women sang and danced as they prepared the evening meal. They too were dressed in reptile skins and were oddly beautiful compared to the men. They were small and petite with pretty faces and slender bodies. They smiled as they sang and placed steaming bowls of food upon a serving table. The benches were carved into the walls of the room and here brightly lit torches hung on the walls above them. The women were busily placing empty bowls and utensils upon these benches when they all turned to look as Bjork and Morgan and the fairies entered. Suddenly the room fell silent. Each Cavedweller young and old stood or sat frozen, staring in wonder before Morgan spoke. "It's alright my people, these strangers are our guests. It is with great joy that I introduce you to Bjork the Hork and his Nimbus fairy men. Nimrod, Jacor, Ryob, Mahew and Jeziah." As he spoke each in turn stepped forward and gave a quick bow." Please make them feel welcome for I know not when we'll have another opportunity to entertain visitors." With his last remark, the cave dwellers smiled and immediately went back to their work and play. The music and laughter grew louder as the old cave dwellers each introduced themselves and sat down at one long bench with Morgan. "Bjork you requested to hear everything about us now is your chance. Come sit with us, the oldest cave dwellers and I shall enjoy telling you, but first let's eat." he gestured to an empty spot upon the bench beside him. Morgan removed his helmet and armor and placed them on a rock shelf behind him. Bjork sat down as the women folk began serving the steaming bowls of delicious hot stew. There was also a sparkling spring water to wash it all down. Everything was so good and Bjork was more hungry than he thought so he ate until he could hold no more. "That was truly delicious, what do you call it?" he asked." Prairie dog hash, (one of my personal favorites)" Morgan said. Bjork looked a little green after that; he'd never eaten such a thing before. Morgan laughed and slapped his hand upon the bench table. Instantly a woman appeared carrying a large flask. "We only use this for special occasions," Morgan said." Empty stone mugs were then filled with the most delicious wine Bjork had ever tasted. "May I inquire what we are drinking?" he asked. Morgan took a sip and said," Elderberry wine my friend." "50 years ago my ancestors lived upon the land which was lush with trees, flowers and covered with elderberry bushes. They stored their wine down here in the cool dark caves for fermentation. When the Sandserpents appeared and began devouring the nutrients that were in the soil, my ancestors began to grow strawberries, and other vegetation down here in the large garden chamber where we do receive a few rays of sunlight from above. They watered their plants with the natural spring water that forms in the pools of the cave floor. Then as the land turned harsh and became barren my ancestors were forced to permanently move underground. At that time they had ample supplies of the wine still left. We only open a flask now and then to celebrate and to preserve what we have left. We live on the fruits of their garden, which we work in daily and the prairie dogs that we hunt at dusk once a month, which is the only time spent up above. It is this that sustains us. Our ancestors were very wise to provide for the future. We are relatively safe down here, but on occasion a Sandserpent will find it's way inside and that is why I was making my journey through the passages and ran into you, Bjork." he laughed. "Or rather you ran into me, didn't you?" Bjork smiled and nodded his head. The Elderberry wine was beginning to have its effects on him and soon he found himself singing and dancing with the Cave dwellers. The celebration went on for quite sometime and then Morgan spoke with a slur" Forgive me my friend I believe I have drank my full share of wine tonight, you must be tired, allow me to show you to your sleeping chamber." He swung his arm out in a pointing motion to a dimly lit path to the left of them, and Bjork wearily and perhaps a little unsteady on his feet followed, humming a tune with the night's music still in his ears. The Nimbus fairy men flew along behind with their sacks of Juju berries, all but Ryob who was busy trying to woo some young female cavedwellers.

"Ryob, I hate to interrupt your conversation, but we are all retiring for the evening", Nimrod said. "Very well Nimrod, good evening fair ladies," Ryob said as he bowed, grabbed his sack and then began following Nimrod.

Morgan led them down into a large chamber where stone cots were carved in the walls and covered with thick reptilian skin for comfort. Here Bjork lie down and soon fell fast asleep (while visions of dancing Cavedweller women filled his head). How he longed to see his Naomi he thought, how beautiful she was. No one could compare, no one. The chambers echoed with Bjork's snoring and the cave dweller's loud breathing. The fairies rested as they kept watch. They had learned to never take anything for granted. That Sandserpent had frightened them all. It was such a large scaly beast. Yet it did serve its purpose; supplying the skins for clothing, armor, and furnishings .It was strange how they had taken so much from the Cave dwellers and yet given so much in return.

Bjork slept like a log and when he awoke he felt truly refreshed. He sat on the edge of his cot and smiled to himself. The sweet dreams he had were still fresh in his mind, and he was more than ready to start for home. Home he thought, what a wonderful word that is.

Today he would reach her, Naomi. He would give her the cure and she would awaken to live a long life, beautiful, and eternally his. He could smell the familiar flowers of the Nimbus meadow and feel the brush of the butterfly wings as they traveled from flower to flower pollinating each one, giving each a new life. Just as his cure would give new life to Naomi. The sun would be shining and the birds would be singing and his heart would be pounding with the pure joy of the day!

"Nimbus fairies today is the day we go home!" he exclaimed. "Let us hurry!" With that he was up and out the chamber doorway and rushing up the path to bid farewell to his Cavedweller friends. He could smell the cooking of sweetbreads as he rushed into the eating room. Morgan was sitting at his bench, and looked well rested now. He waved to Bjork to join him. "You look well my friend, come eat, talk awhile before you leave us". Bjork sat down and soon he had a hot mug of frothing cider and a slice of thick sweetbread placed before him. He ate ravenously as he told Morgan the story of Naomi's plight and of his adventures to cure her. Morgan sat still, a very captive audience, fully enjoying the stories. When Bjork had finished he rose and said, " I am so sorry that I can't stay longer, but as you know I must return with the cure right away."
 "No need for apologies my friend, I would let nothing stand in the way of saving my dear Riana," Morgan said and nodded to his beautiful wife that had prepared the meal." Riana, bring my friends some flasks of spring water, it gets very hot up above this time of day," he said. Soon she reappeared with 5 full flasks in tow. Bjork grabbed them and slipped two in his pockets. Then Nimrod, Jacor and Jeziah placed one

each in theirs. Morgan stood up and said, "Follow me quickly and I will show you the way to the entrance of the cave. Stay close as the paths do tend to wind some. They followed Morgan at a much faster pace now, and soon were at the top, a little out of breath from the steady upward climb. As they began to see the rays of light they hurried even faster. Soon they stood at the entrance .They didn't want to meet up with the Sandserpents today. They must hurry through this desolate land to reach the border. " Thank you for your generosity and thoughtfulness, "Bjork said "I will think of you often. Morgan looked sad as he spoke" If you ever travel this way again be sure to drop in". as he shook Bjork's hand. With that they were through the entrance and hurrying along the dusty paths of Endure that lead home. They only stopped to take a drink from their flasks. Morgan had told them the Sandserpents mainly hunted at night. But still they kept a watch out. The sun was getting lower and the evening getting cooler when they saw the distinct image of a forest off in the distance (Wisteria!). "Hurry we can reach home before nightfall," Bjork cried. His heart was pounding wildly as he ran along the sandy paths.

CHAPTER SEVEN

THE HOMECOMING

Bjork could see the forest edge getting much closer now and was filled with excitement. His mouth felt parched and dry, but he only licked his lips and wiped his sweaty brow. He wouldn't stop to drink until they were safely across the border. He looked behind him and could see the sun setting quickly over the dry desolate horizon of Endure. It had a strange yet beautiful red glow as it lit up the evening sky. The Nimbus fairies were keeping a close watch out for any signs of danger. They kept as near to Bjork as possible, carrying their sacks of Juju berries. Bjork heard a strange sound off to his right and could distinctly see the rising of the sandy earth. It rose as if about to explode, forming a large hill not too far from where he was now standing. He peered at it in curiosity for a moment and then it was Jeziah that spoke. "I believe we're not alone out here!" he mumbled as he grabbed Bjork and attempted to raise him off the ground. With the weight of the berries and only one hand free and Bjork being quite a bit heavier than a fairy man, he didn't succeed. It was then that the ground opened wide and Bjork felt another tug on his other arm as Nimrod swiftly came to their rescue. Bjork passed within inches of the awful Sandserpent and now understood the horror of meeting one head on. Its head was over 2 feet wide, with an even larger gaping, hissing mouth, and two long protruding fangs. It raised it's body in an attempt to reach it's prey, but fell short and now remained hissing , awaiting any creature that dared to cross it's path.

Bjork's heart was beating wildly as the Nimbus fairies made a rapid flight to the safety of the Wisteria forest. Only the rippling creek that lay on the other side prevented the Sandserpents from entering in. It was as if there was an invisible shield or barrier, which separated the two distinctly different lands.

The Sandserpents had evolved in the arid climate of Endure and could not tolerate water, nor could they swim against the creek's fast running currents. Here from the sparkling waters had they filled their flasks when their journey began. How odd it was also, Bjork thought that the climate changed so drastically in such a short distance. It was cool and comfortable here and Bjork felt calm at last. "Let's rest awhile. I feel suddenly so thirsty, "he spoke. They all agreed. The sun was now completely set and they could hear the sounds of the Hork's and their children at play. They could see the smoke from their campfire and it's flickering light that was reflected upon the forest trees and rocks that stood nearby. The owls began their evening serenade, as they entered the clearing and stood at last safe again upon Wisteria ground.

The Hork's young and old alike rushed to greet them. The children stared with curiosity. An older gentleman stepped forward. "Is this Bjork and his fairies that have returned at last from their dangerous journeys? "He squinted trying to see better.
"Yes, it is I", Bjork said. " I'm back in Hork Land and not a moment too soon!" They soon found themselves in the middle of a large group of Horks (each of them shouting out questions, excitedly awaiting answers.) "All in time my people, "Bjork spoke with command. "I have a much more important task unfinished, the entire reason for our travels. I will tell all when I have finished the task at hand. But tonight belongs to Naomi. With that I bid you adieu", he bowed and curtseyed and raised his arms majestically as he deeply thought of Naomi's Meadow. The gowns powers felt stronger than ever to him as he called out,
 "Hurry Nimrod! I pray we are not too late!".

Nimrod and Jacor quickly flew in the direction of the meadow. "Naomi lives still, I can feel it in my soul," Nimrod spoke.

The Nimbus fairies were well known for their mental telepathy. They were able to communicate feelings of pain, loss and joy. "I would have felt her go," he said. Bjork's mind was filled with anxiety, as deep in concentration he waited impatiently for the gowns powers to transport him to Naomi. He didn't notice when the sun began shining, or the birds singing, nor did he notice the other Nimbus fairies that flew by. But a strange stabbing pain in his heart rendered him conscious, as he now could hear the sound of weeping fairies. He looked through their midst, and there she was, prone on her bed, her eyes closed tight. Beside her as if made of stone sat her father Caliope the Nimbus Fairy King. Bjork wanted to scream out, but he held his breath instead.

Nimrod and Jacor who had arrived brought him gently to his feet beside her. His pain was so intense, his eyes were brimming with tears, as he leaned his head forward and strained to see if her chest was moving. Was she no longer breathing? Was he too late? He couldn't see the rise and fall of her bosom, nor hear the shallow breaths. He cried out to Nimrod, "But you said you knew she was still alive! How could you be so wrong?"

Nimrod looked puzzled as he spoke, "I can't be wrong, I can't...As his eyes filled with glistening fairy tears. Caliope immediately raised to his feet a look of deep remorse and shock upon his face. And spoke" I too cannot be wrong, he said," Can I Nimrod my son?" I have sat here faithfully by her side awaiting your return, how could I not feel this? How could I not know?" "I know I have lost many of my powers, but of this I am certain I would feel her passing," and he sadly sat back down.

Feeling defeated and full of grief, Bjork laid his head upon her chest. What was this? He listened carefully, yes he was sure it was, her heart was still beating. Very faintly but, yet it definitely was beating. "Hurry Nimrod, crush the juju berries into juice, I hear a faint heartbeat!" he exclaimed.
Caliope hurriedly gave the orders, "Do as he says my people, we must hurry!" The Nimbus fairies that had been crying sprang into action and soon all the berries had been crushed and the juice strained into a flask. Bjork gently pulled Naoimi into a sitting position, with one arm around her and gently pried her lips apart with the other hand." Pour it slowly and don't drown her. Don't spill a drop," he said. They very slowly and very carefully poured the juice in her mouth, as she began to gag and then swallowed. They continued the procedure until all the juice had been drank. Bjork looked for signs of revival, but there was none. Her eyes remained shut, her body limp, as he gently laid her back upon the pillow.
 He knelt down beside her now, holding her hand, silently praying. Nimrod too sat upon her bed and ran his fingers threw her beautiful hair as he called to her," Naomi it is I Nimrod your brother. I bring with me Bjork, "Open your eyes and see for yourself." He repeated this over three times and each time he spoke with such authority as if giving a direct command. He showed no signs of emotion, until Naomi's eyes at last opened, and she wearily sat up. "Excuse me brother, Bjork, how long have I been sick?" She knew that fairies never slept, but did lose consciousness when ill."

For quite some time, dear sister," said Nimrod as he
picked her up in his arms and gaily flew around." "I'm
so glad to see you're feeling better." "We will tell you
of our adventure, but please in the future don't travel
away from home, without a companion. She stared at
him in puzzlement and looked equally surprised by
Bjork's appearance. He looked extremely happy, but
she was sure that he had been crying. How odd she
thought. Her father too, whom she had not seen shed
a tear since the day her Mother was taken, was now
crying openly and held out his arms to welcome her
embrace. She quickly ran to him feeling his pain."
Father, Father what's wrong?" she asked." My child
nothing is wrong, not anymore," he said as he hugged
her, "everything is perfect now." Bjork thought she
looked more beautiful than ever. He too hugged her
closely, perhaps tighter than he ever had. Then he
stepped back. Suddenly he felt so very, very tired.
Nimrod noticed and said, "We will tell you everything
tomorrow Naomi, but for now I think we should send
our weary friend home." I can never repay you for the
debt I owe you Bjork", Caliope said. "But now my
friend go home and rest, sleep well as all Hork's do, "
he added, as he patted him on the back.
  HOME Bjork thought, oh yes, HOME, in his own
comfortable bed. He touched the folds of his green
gown and thought of his bedroom that lay inside his
cozy house. Miraculously within moments he found
himself transported there, snuggled in his blankets,
lying on his own bed his head upon his own soft
pillow. It was as though he had never left Home. Had
this all been a dream he thought? An old Hork's mind
can play tricks on him. He was far too exhausted to
think right now. I'll contemplate this tomorrow he
thought. In his weary stupor, he yawned through

blurry eyes. He didn't notice the large new book that lay on his bedside table , or that on its cover was written "Tales of a Wimpet King". Soon he was sound and deep asleep as the walls of his home echoed with the sounds of his patterned breathing.

TO BE
CONTINUED...
....

Made in the USA
Charleston, SC
10 March 2013